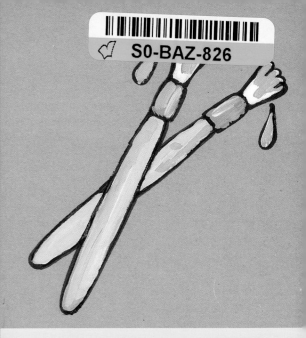

What do Sarah and the other children play with at school?

What do they eat at school?

What does Sarah take to school with her?

What do Sarah and her classmates look for outside?

Which chair is Sarah's?

First published in Belgium and Holland by Clavis Uitgeverij, Hasselt – Amsterdam, 2011
Copyright © 2011, Clavis Uitgeverij

English translation from the Dutch by Clavis Publishing Inc. New York
Copyright © 2016 for the English language edition: Clavis Publishing Inc. New York

Visit us on the web at www.clavisbooks.com

Sarah Goes to School written and illustrated by Pauline Oud
Original title: *Saar gaat naar school*
Translated from the Dutch by Clavis Publishing

ISBN 978-1-60537-259-4

This book was printed in April 2016 at Publikum d.o.o., Slavka Rodica 6, Belgrade, Serbia

First Edition
10 9 8 7 6 5 4 3 2 1

Sarah
Goes to School

Pauline Oud

Clavis

NEW YORK

"Come on, Sarah," Mom says.
"It's time to go to school."
Sarah quickly finds her scarf and jacket.
Mom already has her backpack.

"You're so quick,"
Mom says, laughing.
"That's me!" Sarah says.

Mom takes Sarah to school.
"Bye, Sarah," Mom says at
the school gate.
Sarah waves as she runs
to her friends.

There is Lisa!
And Adam!
And... a boy who
Sarah has never
seen before.
He is a new
student.

BRRIING! There goes the bell!
The children walk into the school
and take off their coats.
Sarah hangs her coat under the picture
of the flower. That is her picture.
Adam hangs his coat under the picture
of the boat. That is his picture.
The new boy doesn't have
a picture yet. His mom
helps him take off his
coat.

In the classroom Sarah sits on the chair with the flower.
"This is my chair," she says to the new boy.
"Good morning," Ms. Anne says when everyone is seated in a circle.
"Today is a very special day, because we have a new boy in our class! Do you want to tell us your name?"
"Ian," the new boy says quietly.
Sarah thinks it is a beautiful name.

After the teacher has read a story it's time to play!
Ian gets to pick first:
He wants to play in the building corner.
"Come with me," Sarah says, and takes
Ian to where the blocks are.
Together they build a beautiful tower.

Lisa and Adam play in the house corner.
Adam makes delicious soup in the kitchen,
and Lisa puts the doll to sleep.

"I have to pee," Ian says suddenly.
The teacher takes Ian to the toilet.
Sarah goes along, because she has to pee too.
"Ms. Anne doesn't pee here," Sarah tells Ian.

"She has her own toilet. It's a big one.
Just like at home."
When Ian and Sarah are done,
they wash their hands at the sink.
"Come on," Sarah says.
"Let's go back to class."

When Sarah and Ian return to the classroom, the other children are at the table waiting for them.
Sarah puts her chair with the flower at the big table.
Ian sits next to her on the chair with the tree.
The tree is now his picture.

Ms. Anne has put fruit and juice on the table
for the children's snack.
After snack time the children sing songs.
First Sarah picks a song. Then Ian and Lisa pick one.

Now it's time to play outside. "Bring your coat!"
Sarah tells Ian.
In the playground there's a slide and a sandbox.
There are also wagons and bikes.
Sarah quickly runs to a wagon. "Come on," she calls to Ian.

Ian gets the first turn.
He is an excellent driver!

"Come, children," Ms. Anne calls.
"Look at these. Do you know what they are?"
"They're leaves!" the children call out together.
"They come from the tree,"
Sarah says, and she nods at Ian.
"That's right," the teacher says.
"Now you go and collect some leaves. There are lots on the ground. Do you see them?" Sarah picks up a beautiful orange leaf. Ian finds a leaf that is big and green.

Back in
the classroom
the children
make special
things with the
leaves they found
outside.

Sarah makes a beautiful painting.
"This is for Ian," she says.
Ian makes a nice crown.
"I am the king,"
he says proudly.

After painting and cutting and pasting it is time to clean up. Ian sweeps the floor with a broom. It is Adam's turn to water the plants. He is very careful. And Sarah? She cleans up the paint. "You are excellent helpers," the teacher says happily. "That's us!" Sarah says.

Sarah's mom is already waiting.
Ian's, Lisa's, and Adam's moms
and dads are there too.
"There's a new boy in my class,"
Sarah tells her mom.
"His name is Ian and he is my friend."
"Bye, Sarah," Ian calls.
"See you tomorrow!"

"Bye, school. Bye, everyone," Sarah says, and waves.
"See you tomorrow!"